Becoming the Aliens' Egg-Laying Hucow

BLAIR AJAX

Find more erotic stories by Blair Ajax at:
https://BlairAjax.com

Chapter 1: If Only

The metal door in front of me hisses open, revealing the medical bay. I step in and look around for the ship's doctor, my boyfriend Jeremy.

"Yes, Elena, come in. You're right on time for your treatment," he says.

"My treatment?" I must have totally forgotten. But then, why *am* I here?

"Please take off your uniform and take a seat."

So he wants to play doctor and patient, does he? Well, this is rather kinky.

With a smile on my lips I step to my left toward one of the six beige-padded medical examination beds that protrude from the wall. Each one has a medical readout screen above it that are currently deactivated.

Reaching up to the zipper on the front of my skin-tight shiny dark-blue uniform, I pull it down. Almost instantly, I'm naked and sitting sideways on the medical bed with my legs dangling over the side.

Doctor Jeremy approaches me, in his similar style uniform but with a white lab-coat on top of it.

"So doctor, what's my treatment?" I say as I reach out and run my finger down his svelte chest and abs, toward the bulge that's near his groin.

"Impregnation," he answers matter-of-factly, but with a slight smirk on his lips. My heart leaps, and my vagina clenches once as it begins to become wet.

He unzips his uniform down as far as it goes, and his rock-hard penis jumps right out.

"But we're not supposed to—"

"I've gotten special permission from Captain Kriger. It will be nine months before you're ready to deliver, and we'll be back on Earth in seven months. So it's no problem."

I lean back and spread my legs. He steps forward, placing his hands under my thighs. Thanks to the medical bed, my pussy is at the exact same height as his cock, so his stiff dick immediately finds my slick hole and penetrates me.

"Oh, doctor!" I exclaim, as I feel him push deeper and deeper into me.

He smiles at me and his green eyes sparkle. I reach up and run my hand through his curly dark hair while he begins to thrust.

This is just so incredibly satisfying! You wouldn't believe how horny I've been over the last three-and-a-half years of this deep-space exploration mission. Especially since I hit it off with the ship's sexy doctor, and we've been dating for nearly that entire time.

"Oh, yes, oh, that's so good!" I mumble.

Tilting my head back so that it hangs off the other side of the medical bed, my long ponytail dangles in mid-air. My entire body jostles back and forth while Jeremy pounds my pussy.

I reach up and tweak my nipples, as I imagine what I'll look like once I'm pregnant. I hope my now-moderate boobs will get maybe twice as big, or even bigger! I'll be so sexy with a huge pregnant belly. Maybe I'll have triplets? *Quadruplets*, even!

Jeremy groans as he keeps fucking me, and I savor the pleasure we've both longed for. I can't believe it's finally happening, and it's better than I ever expected! All I need now is for him to inseminate me...

"Ah, oh, ohhh, yes, YES! Jeremy, make me pregnant," I cry out. "So very, *very* pregnant!"

"*Ohhhhh…*" he groans, and his throbbing cock unleashes a blast of cum. His semen surges up through my cervix and into my womb.

"More! Oh, give me *more!*" I cry out. My vagina grips his veiny throbbing shaft, as if it wants to milk him for every last drop he's got.

He doesn't disappoint. One load of semen after another enters my body, and my ecstasy continues.

Somehow, the doctor just keeps cumming in me! Oh yeah, I'm *definitely* going to get pregnant.

In fact, as I tilt my head up, my lower tummy is already bulging. But how can I be this pregnant already? Oh fuck, I don't care—I've wanted to have his baby ever since I met him!

"You're going to be a wonderful mother to our sextuplets," Jeremy says, still ejaculating into me with everything he's got.

Sextuplets! OH *YES!* My orgasm continues, sending waves of pleasure throughout my body, while my belly just keeps growing bigger, and *bigger*.

The medical monitor attached to the bed turns on and starts to beep loudly, but by now, I'm probably as big as a full-term pregnancy, and Jeremy is *still* spewing his semen into my womb.

I close my eyes to savor the feeling. But *damn*, won't that annoying beeping just shut off already?!

Reaching to the side, I slap my hand against the monitor, and finally, it shuts off.

Suddenly, it's all gone. The panel built into the wall next to my head has several large numbers glowing faint blue. 06:33.

I let out a loud sigh, and run my hands down my flat abdomen. I'm not pregnant, it was all just a dream. Damn.

Still, it was fucking hot. I reach my hand down my loose pajama shorts and stick my middle finger between my folds.

Oh yeah, I'm wet. *Really* wet. But there's no time to masturbate. I need to get dressed and head down to the shuttlebay to start running my pre-flight checks before I take a team of researchers down to the new planet we began orbiting late yesterday evening.

"Ugggh," I groan as I roll out of my bunk and stumble into the small cramped bathroom attached to my tiny quarters. In here there's just a sink, commode, and walk-in shower stall. Outside I've got three drawers for personal things built into the wall opposite my bunk.

I know I shouldn't complain. It's better than having to share a bunkroom with several other women, and I totally understand that this ship isn't designed for luxury. Fortunately, the designers were at least smart enough to realize that nearly four years without even a tiny slice of privacy would psychologically bother most people.

And I shouldn't complain about my job, either. Being out here on the very edges of known space is a privilege that most people don't have. Plus, I get to have the fun of flying my shuttle down to brand-new planets every few weeks as our ship catalogs new systems and makes preliminary surveys of what we discover. This is paving the way for the scientists back on Earth to choose which planets are worthy of establishing a longer-term scientific outpost on.

I pull off my loose black t-shirt and shorts and toss them out the bathroom door where they land on my bunk, then step into the shower.

Instantly, hot water flows down over me, and the screen built into the shower stall's wall ahead of me starts showing me the initial overnight scans of the planet, and the region that the Alpha research team wants to explore first. It looks to be near the planet's equator, on a continent with dense green vegetation.

Although I should be looking for good potential landing spots nearby, I just can't get my sexy dream out of my head. Why did Captain Kriger have to forbid anyone from having sex on board?

Sure, I can see the problems it might lead to. We certainly wouldn't want people to start shacking up with each other and causing drama. Plus, the ship definitely isn't meant to handle families, and even one toddler running around the corridors would be total chaos.

Now that we're nearing the end of our four-year mission though, maybe Jeremy really could ask the captain for permission for us to start trying? Of course, first I'll have to ask Jeremy if he's okay with giving up his space-exploration career to raise a family. But if he loves me and wants me to be happy, I don't see why he'd disagree. I'll have to bring it up sometime.

The image of how big my belly was in my dream comes back into my mind, and my clit twinges. Sextuplets really would be perfect.

Okay, there's no way I'll be able to focus until I do this—I can look for a landing spot later. Slipping a finger down between my legs, I start to rub my clit. My left hand grabs the safety-bar, and I lean back against the shower stall while the warm water flows down over me.

I've never even seen Jeremy's cock in real life. But I bet he's got a good-sized one. Maybe it really would feel as good as in my dream?

If only he could be in here with me, and could press his sexy naked body up against mine. He could lift me up, and drive his erection right into my pussy as he holds me against the shower wall.

Then, I'd kiss him while I wrap my arms around his strong shoulders, and he'd thrust nice and hard. I'd feel the head of his cock sliding back and forth inside my tunnel, and then, it would erupt and send his seed straight into—

"Yes, YES! OH, oh yeah, oh… Jeremy, impregnate me," I cry out. My legs tremble and I grip the safety-bar to hold myself up while my orgasm tapers off.

Taking a deep breath, I open my eyes. Damn, that was too short. But the screen says it's 06:48? I need to start my pre-flight checks by 07:00 sharp!

Quickly, I grab a handful of body-gel from the wall-mounted dispenser and begin to lather myself up. I make sure to rinse out my pussy too, and then turn on the shower's automatic-dry function. Warm air blows out of the corners of the stall, evaporating all the water from my skin.

My hair is still slightly damp when I press stop on the shower's display screen, but I don't have time for more. I won't even have time for breakfast at this rate, but once we land I'll have time for a snack.

I rush out of the shower and tug open my drawer to find a clean pair of panties and a fresh stretchy blue unitard. As soon as I zip it up, I throw my hair back into my usual ponytail and rush out of my quarters.

Chapter 2: My Encounter

"Alright everyone, head out. Report back here by 15:30 sharp," Gerald, our team's lead researcher, instructs. The ten members of the research team that I'd brought down in my shuttle begin to fan out and head away from the shore of the large lake that was the only viable landing spot near their desired exploration site.

I turn back toward my shuttle and step through the open rear hatch. Along each wall are a number of fold-down seats with harnesses that the research team used. My seat and a spot for the lead researcher are up at the front.

I reach into the mesh pocket on the back of my seat to pull out the metal pre-prepared meal kit. Sure, it's only 09:12, and too early for lunch, but my stomach is grumbling. If only I hadn't spent so much time masturbating I might have had time to stop by the cafeteria and grab a filling protein smoothie.

Now, though, I'll have to get by with a canteen of electrolyte-infused vitamin water, and a few dense energy bars. At least this should do since I just have to sit around here all day while I wait for the researchers to return from their scouting expedition.

Grabbing my snack, I head back out of the shuttle and take a seat on a large rock near the shore.

The lake here is a gorgeous shade of turquoise that contrasts nicely with the reddish-orange rocks and coarse sand. The sky above is a pale green with only a few high wispy clouds.

After gulping down the last few bites of my energy bar, I take a swig of the fruity-flavored water. But I should save this for later. Putting it back in the metal box, I head back into the shuttlecraft to drop the box back in the mesh pocket behind my pilot's seat.

I run my finger under the collar of my unitard, and it comes back wet with sweat. Damn, it's hot out. I know it's a tropical jungle, but the humidity is really getting to me. Inside the shuttle is starting to feel like an oven.

Of course, this is a nice change from the last planet we were on. It was just at the outer edge of its star's habitable zone. I had to wear bulky insulated pants and a matching jacket while I hunkered down inside the shuttle, keeping the power on just enough so that the fuel lines didn't freeze up. But of course I had to go out regularly and clear off the blowing ice crystals from the air intake vents, and that wasn't fun at all.

At least this part of this planet is warm, and it's certainly beautiful. It might not hurt to go for a little walk around the edge of the lake. Maybe, if I can get a little privacy, I could even go for a swim! I've certainly got the time to kill.

Off to my left maybe three-quarters of a mile away the lake seems to continue around a small mountain. That should give me enough privacy for a little skinny-dipping.

Just in case, I grab my personal handheld scanner, so that as I walk I can keep a lookout for any approaching life-forms that could be dangerous. Leaving the shuttle behind, I start out for a hike along the shore of the lake.

When I make it to a place where I can see around the small mountain, I'm thrilled to spot a stunning waterfall spilling over the edge of the reddish-orange cliff only a few hundred feet away. The waterfall lands on a cluster of large boulders. Other boulders that must have fallen off the cliff in the past form a small ridge that separates part of the lake into a smaller pool that's fed by the waterfall. It looks perfect!

With a smile on my face, I take in a breath of the fragrant tropical air and stride with excitement toward the pool. Once here, I choose a large dry boulder at the edge of the pool and put my scanner down on it. I unzip my unitard and peel it off, taking my feet out of the built-in shoes, and place it onto the rock also. My white panties are soon added to the pile.

From my earlier scans, the water is just plain old water with some minerals that add the turquoise color. When I dip my toes in, I can't help but smile. The cooling water is even more wonderful as I walk out deeper into it, my feet pushing through the coarse sand that lines the bottom of the pool.

Oh yeah, now this hits the spot! The warmth of the air keeps me from being cold, but the water is so refreshing. I haven't been swimming since I left Earth nearly three-and-a-half years ago!

Soon, I'm deep enough that I can actually start to swim a little. I paddle back and forth across the small pool, enjoying the feeling of the water on my bare skin.

It's too bad that Jeremy is stuck up on the ship. Otherwise, if he were here, it'd be the perfect spot to sneak in a quick fucking. After all, technically, we wouldn't be *on board*, now would we?

Damn, how sexy would it be if he could fuck me out here? When we're back on Earth I could tell all my friends about it. They would surely *ooh* and *ahh* over my story of how me and my sexy doctor husband conceived our first child while skinny-dipping in a tropical alien paradise!

But that same horniness I had this morning comes back to me. I swim back toward shore and lay down on the sand at the edge of the water. The small ripples from the waterfall lap at the underside of my breasts as I reach down and start to gently touch my perky clit.

Oh yeah, this is good. I can just imagine Jeremy on top of me, his cock buried in my pussy, thrusting inside me as we fuck on this alien beach, while I just wait for his fertile load to be unleashed.

Beep-beep, beep-beep, beep beep.

Dammit, not now! But what is my scanner detecting?

To my left, I notice movement by the cliff, behind the waterfall. My heart leaps as three large teal-skinned humanoid beings emerge through the waterfall, then climb over some of the boulders to get down toward the pool below.

Fuck, they're *aliens*—they must be! But I need to shut off my scanner now before they hear it beeping!

Yet somehow, I'm too stunned to move. The pit of my stomach fills with dread as one of them looks in my direction. It points toward me with one of its muscular arms and makes a long 'ooooo' sound, and the other two also turn to look.

They don't seem to have any weapons with them. They're also all totally naked, and appear to be completely bald. Still, each one is as well-built as the most muscular human men I've ever seen. If they're hostile, I could still be in a lot of trouble, so I'd better not do anything to startle them or make them think I'm a threat.

Finally, I will myself to stand up and grab my scanner off the boulder, and fumble for the button to shut it off. My heart is racing as the three strong aliens slowly head toward me.

Now that they're only thirty feet away, I can notice some unusual features. They don't seem to have ears, but the two small suction-cup-like formations that protrude on small stalks from their upper foreheads look like they could be an alternative. Their mouths are surrounded by a perfect O-shaped ring of protruding teal lips. I don't hear any words, but each one is emitting a strange series of little melodic tones. Is that how they talk?

My gaze progresses downward, over their strong pectorals, eight-pack abs, and settles on the largest penises I've ever seen! Under them are equally-large, totally bald alien scrotums. They might even have *three* testicles in there?

My clit pulses at the sight of their alien cocks. I know I should probably flee back to my shuttle and contact the captain to tell him I've discovered aliens that look to be equivalent in intelligence to humans. Despite this, I can't make myself turn away.

I can't believe I'm just standing here as three huge alien men are coming slowly toward me, still making a series of strange tones without words.

"But I don't know what you're saying," I say softly, trying to not to do anything that might startle them.

As they get closer and closer, I watch with awe as their penis-heads emerge from inside their alien foreskins, and their cocks become erect.

So they're getting turned on by *me? Really?* Three alien men think I'm hot?

Even though the aliens are only ten feet away from me now, I'm not feeling as scared as

I was before. Their little musical tones are actually sort of cute, and those huge dicks are definitely something else. The aliens seem peaceful, and are probably just curious about me. I know I'm *definitely* curious about them.

I can feel my vagina pulsating gently the longer I look at them. What would one of those big alien penises feel like in me? I admit I'm still rather horny from my interrupted masturbation session, and now, I'm just so incredibly tempted.

Jeremy never has to find out, right? Technically, he's not even my fiancé. I haven't even had sex with him, so really, he has no right to tell me I can't fuck these aliens if I want to.

Slowly, I begin to approach the three alien men.

The captain would surely be upset if he discovered that I've fucked an alien, though. We're given strict rules about what to do if we contact intelligent alien life, and having sex with them on the beach certainly isn't part of that. But if the captain had only been a bit more reasonable with his rules, I wouldn't be as incredibly horny as I am now. So it's all his fault, really.

The aliens stop moving, and we're standing only feet from each other. I look them up and down, and I'm sure they're over eight feet tall!

I purse my lips and tentatively reach out a hand toward the alien's chest. I put my palm on his strong pectoral, then slowly run my hand over it. I'm amazed by how smooth his skin feels. I bring up my other hand and continue to run my palms over his amazing body.

Slowly, he lifts up his large teal hand that has strange little bulbs on the end of each of his six fingers. He runs it over my wet hair, and pulls the end of my wet ponytail over my shoulder.

From here, he touches my shoulder, then moves across to my collarbone.

"Mmm hmm," I say, trying to tell him that I'm okay with his touch.

The other aliens step around to either side of me, and now I'm surrounded. Each one begins to gently run their fingers over my naked body.

The alien in front of me brings up his other hand, and runs his bulbous fingers down over my breasts, until he cups them. His thumbs make contact with my nipples, and it just feels so sexy to be here being touched by these hot alien men.

But I already want more. I reach down and take his erect cock in my hand. I'm amazed that I can't even close my fingers around his girth. He's also probably at least ten inches long.

Gently, I begin to slide my hand up and down his cock. He emits a few little tones. This must feel good for him?

I look up at his face, and give him a closed-mouth smile, just in case showing my teeth might look aggressive. He still doesn't respond.

Okay, well, here goes. I slowly squat down in front of him until my lips are at the height of his cock. Slowly, I begin to kiss his knob, which is a little more rounded than I'd expect, but still similar enough to a human one.

I move my lips over his knob, and even up the side of his shaft. He doesn't move, but his shaft throbs a few times under my hand. Looking up at him, his eyes are closed, and even if his weird O-shaped mouth means he can't smile, the longer tones he's making sound pleasurable to me.

I open my mouth and manage to fit his bulbous knob inside, where I tease it with my tongue. Then I start sucking on it.

"Ooo, oo-oooo, ooo," he says in a few different pitches. I feel his hands on my shoulders, and I take his dick out of his mouth and look up at him. What does he want?

He raises both his hands upward, and so I stand up. Now to my surprise, he bends down, and puts his O-shaped lips on my right nipple.

His sudden suction makes me gasp with pleasure.

"Oh, that's *nice*," I say softly.

The alien to my left stops feeling me up once he notices what the first one is doing. He shifts into position and also puts his mouth over my left nipple, and sucks.

My clit twinges from the amazing sensations their unusual O-shaped lips are bringing me. I *definitely* want to try one of their alien cocks in me. But the aliens just keep sucking on my nipples, making me wetter and wetter, and causing me to moan gently.

But after a few minutes they suddenly stop. Okay, now's my chance to show them what I *really* want.

I quickly sit down and lean back so that I'm lying on the coarse reddish-orange sand. The alien behind me moves out of the way, and all three of the teal-skinned aliens just stand there and watch me. Spreading my legs, I reveal my soaking-wet pussy to them, and point at it.

"Fuck me," I say. But I remember they can't understand me.

However, the two aliens standing next to the first alien squat down on either side of me and put their hands on my shoulder and my torso. They bend over and once again fix their O-shaped lips around my nipples and begin to suck. I guess they really like my tits.

Fortunately, the third alien squats between my legs, and he pushes his large teal fingers through my labia a little. Just when I'm hoping he gets the idea, he also bends forward, puts his hands on my spread thighs, and fastens his mouth over my clit.

"Ah, oh! Oh!" I exclaim, as the intense sensation on my bean surprises me. Immediately, he reduces his suction.

Now that's the perfect amount. His round lips tug on my bean at just the right frequency that my vagina starts clenching, and I'm sure I'm totally dripping down there with arousal.

I never would have believed anyone if they'd told me this morning that by not even noon, I'd be receiving such bodily pleasure from three alien men on an alien beach!

"Oh yes, oh, oh that's so nice," I moan. I've never had any of my past boyfriends be as interested in sucking on my nipples as these aliens are, or suck my clit in the way the third alien is doing. It feels totally fantastic, but what I *really* want is one of their huge dicks in my hole, right now!

I reach up over the teal heads of the two aliens sucking on my boobs, and gently push the head of the alien who's eating me out. He releases his suction on my clit and looks up at me.

Using my fingers, I make a ring with my left hand, and stick my right pointer finger through it, moving it back and forth several times, then point to my pussy again. Do I really have to explain this to him? Clearly, they've got cocks, and so the females of their species must have pussies, right?

But he's still standing there looking clueless. I tap the heads of the other two aliens, and they take their mouths off of my nipples and also sit up to look at me.

Now, I sit up and reach forward to grasp the cock of the alien who's standing between my spread legs. I tug on it, and he bends down, allowing me to guide his smooth, huge alien cock between my folds. He leans forward, and his round knob slips easily up through my super-slick hole, but his girth stretches me quite a bit.

"Yeah, just like that!" I say, as I lean back. The other two aliens immediately re-take their places sucking on my boobs, making my vagina clench.

The alien whose cock is in my pussy lets out a few louder tones, then pushes his dick farther into me.

"Ohhhh, oh, I'm tight," I say. Or else, he's even bigger than I thought he was. Still, it's so utterly satisfying to finally have my vagina full of cock when it's been well over five years since I did it last. At this point I don't even care that it's alien cock.

From the little sounds he's making, I'd guess he's liking it just as much as I am. As I loosen up, he starts thrusting faster, until his round knob bumps into the end of my pussy several times. Based on their stature, I guess I'm probably much smaller than their alien women are, which explains why he can only fit about sixty percent of his huge cock inside me.

Squatting there on the ground with his strong six-fingered hands gripping my hips, he thrusts his hips forward and back, driving his cock back and forth through my tunnel.

Oh yeah, this is just perfect! I love how his thick alien shaft fills me completely, and his knob massages my slick walls with every thrust. I really hope Jeremy's got a cock big enough to satisfy me after this.

"Oh, oh yeah. Oh. Keep going," I say. The alien's moans are getting louder, and his eyes are closed.

Suddenly I feel a strong pulse of his shaft, stronger than any that I've felt before, and pressure up against my cervix. The alien immediately lets out a full-blown *howl* as his cock spews his alien semen straight into my uterus in one long release.

I can't believe it—I've just been inseminated *by an alien!*

"Oh yeah, Yeah. OH, oh that's HOT! FUCK YEAH!" I scream as my pussy clamps down on his massive member, and total ecstasy overtakes me.

Unlike the few times I've done it with guys in the past, the alien doesn't blow multiple times. Instead, he quickly pulls out of me, and to my surprise, the alien to my right lets go of my nipple and swaps places with him.

"Oh, you too? Well, why not?"

Despite the small interruption, once my pussy is again full of throbbing alien cock, my orgasm continues. I'm gasping and moaning here while the three aliens pleasure me, and the second one pounds my pussy.

He too begins to moan. Although my climax is decreasing, his thrusts still feel amazing inside my cunt.

After only a minute, the second alien's orgasmic howl is accompanied by another unusually long blast of cum shooting through my cervix.

"Oh, oh, yes, oh, more, MORE!" I cry out. If only Jeremy could make that much semen, he'd surely be able to knock me up right away!

Before I can even savor it, the second alien pulls his cock out of me, and the third alien takes his place between my legs.

"Go ahead, finish me off," I tell him. For all I know, maybe they always fuck their women in groups of three? It does seem like they've done this before.

His cock fills my pussy just as much as the others had, and likewise, he immediately starts to thrust.

Now that my orgasm is starting to fade, I realize just how bizarre it is that I'm laying here letting aliens empty their enormous loads of cum into my pussy. But even more bizarre is how much I want it. One alien would have been good enough, but three is just so kinky!

His shaft is pulsating fast, and it only takes seconds before he's at his peak. His alien howl echoes off the surrounding rocky cliffs, and my womb is filled with a third large surge of cum.

"Ohhhhhh," I moan, as a dull inner ache begins somewhere deep inside my lower abdomen.

The alien pulls his spent dick out of my vagina, and I just lay here while the last remnants of the extreme pleasure I've just experienced course through my body. There's a deep inner ache from how full my uterus must be of alien cum, but that's even sexier, in a way. Surely, I'd need to have ten or maybe even *twelve* human men cum in me to produce the same volume that these three aliens have.

"Thanks, thanks guys, that was great," I sigh softly, and tap on the heads of the two aliens who are still sucking on my nipples.

They let go and stand up. As I look down, I'm amazed at how inflated my nipples are, and how much darker pink they've turned. They're also super-sensitive when I tweak my tips.

The two aliens to either side of me offer me their hands, and I take them. They help me up, and then begin to pull me toward the cliffs behind the waterfall. Is that where they live?

"Sorry, guys, I can't come with you—I have to get back to the shuttle," I say, as I let go of their hands and step backward.

They tilt their heads sideways, and their little suction-cup ears on stems wiggle slightly. The aliens make several long strings of melodic tones, but I just give them a closed-mouth smile and slowly step backwards toward my clothes resting on the boulder.

Fortunately, the aliens don't seem offended. They simply turn away from me and head back to the waterfall by themselves. Here, they start rinsing themselves off just like they would in a shower.

I breathe a sigh of relief and turn toward my clothes. After slipping on my panties and tugging on my stretchy dark-blue unitard, I begin to head back along the beach in the direction of my shuttle.

As amazing as this encounter was, and despite how I feel some alien cum leaking out of my very well-used pussy, I remind myself that I absolutely *need* to keep this a secret.

Chapter 3: Feeling Kind of Weird

By the time I get back to the shuttle, it's 13:23. I guess the hike had taken longer than I expected, and then there was the alien sex I'd just had, too. No wonder my stomach is rumbling.

Back inside the oven-like shuttle, I take out the rest of my food and scarf it down while sitting outside. I also finish off the last of the fruity vitamin water. Even though I've eaten everything and the stomach rumbling is gone, there's still some faint discomfort in my abdomen.

The research team should be back in about two hours, so that's more than enough time to sit here near the lakeshore and contemplate the incredible experience I've just had.

*　　*　　*

I'm still feeling some sort of deep internal ache as I leave the shuttle bay and head back to my quarters. Maybe it's just hunger? Or gas? Or did I pull a muscle during all that hiking and swimming and fucking?

As soon as I get into my quarters I take a shower to get any of the remnants of the minerals from the alien lake out of my hair, and to wash out some alien cum from between my labia.

During the shower, I notice on the digital screen that I've got a message from Doctor Jeremy. Oh, he wants me to come over to his quarters for private dinner. Yeah, I'm up for that. I send a quick reply, then press the button to shut off the water and trigger the automatic dry function.

Now clean and dry, I step out of the shower. In the mirror above the sink, I notice that my tummy is definitely somewhat bloated. But my boobs look fantastic, even though my nipples are still somewhat inflated from all that sucking earlier.

Stepping back out into my quarters, I throw my used unitard and panties into the automatic laundry drawer under my bunk, and grab fresh ones out of my other drawers.

Fully dressed now, I leave my tiny room and eagerly walk down the corridor to my boyfriend's quarters.

When I get there, I press the button outside his door. It beeps, and I wait for him to answer. He's so lucky that he's been assigned one of the largest quarters on the ship. I suppose being the ship's doctor does earn him that luxury, and I don't mind taking advantage of it. While the cafeteria is alright, and it's great to see my friends, the privacy of his quarters are a nice change of pace.

His door soon hisses open to reveal Jeremy standing there with a smile on his face. I can already smell the food he got as take-out from the cafeteria, and my stomach growls.

"Elena, come in," he says, and I do. Once the door closes I wrap my arms around his neck and tilt my head up to receive his kiss.

I feel kind of weird knowing that he has no idea that I just had sex with three alien men hardly five hours ago. Probably some of their cum is still in my uterus, even though I'm about to have dinner with the man I hope will be the father of my children.

But who hasn't had a little fling at some point in the past? If I tell him now, it'll only make him jealous, or angry, and I don't need that now. I just want *food!*

"Mmm, smells great," I say, and head directly for the small table where he's got two takeout containers of food sitting out, along with cutlery, and glasses of juice.

Hopefully if I'm sitting down, he won't notice the slight bulge on my lower abdomen. The last thing I need from him is another lecture about getting more exercise since being a pilot is a sedentary job.

I take my usual seat, and Jeremy sits opposite me. Grabbing my fork, I dig in. Looks like it was Greek night in the cafeteria, so I've got some flavorful rice, lemon potatoes, salad with olives and feta cheese, and a skewer of roasted chicken.

"Mmmmm," I mumble with a mouthful of rice. "You wouldn't believe how hungry I've been all afternoon," I say after swallowing.

"Yeah? So, what was the planet like?" Jeremy asks.

"Oh, it was beautiful. There was a gorgeous teal lake, and the weather was hot, too. We were right at the equator, and everything but the shoreline was dense jungle. I was bored so I went for a little swim, you know—naked," I say with a seductive smile.

"I wish I could've been there," he says, as his eyes light up at the idea. "No wonder you look fabulous tonight. Fresh air does wonders for people's health, plus natural sunlight. And I have to say, your boobs look fantastic," he says, stuffing another bite of salad into his mouth while eyeing my breasts.

"Do they?" I say, cupping them to push them up and make them look just a little bigger under my tight unitard. Maybe now's the time to ask him what I've been thinking ever since last night.

"So Jeremy, there's something I was thinking about during the time down there," I start. "Since we're only seven months away from being back on Earth, do you think you'd be able to get special permission from Captain Kriger to, uh, start trying? You know, you and me?"

"For a baby?" Jeremy asks, as his eyebrows rise up.

"Yeah. It's been fun exploring space way out here these last few years, but I'm starting to want to start a family," I admit. "I had a dream last night that we fucked, and I've been thinking about it all day."

"But Elena, you're only twenty-six, and I'm barely thirty. We could ask to be reassigned for another four-year mission, and still have plenty of time to have a family after that. It would really be great for my career to have more experience under my belt, and I thought you loved flying shuttles and seeing exotic planets?"

"I do," I say, then let out a disappointed sigh. "Okay, I'll think about it a little more. But can you think about it too?"

"Well, I can, if it's important to you. But I don't think it's the best thing right now," he says.

This disagreement puts a damper on the evening, and we finish our meals without saying much else. I just don't know if I can put up with another four years of tiny cramped quarters, and more importantly, no sex.

Finally, we're done eating. My tummy is still feeling weird, and now, sitting here in silence just seems awkward. Plus, I really am quite tired from today's adventure.

"Would you want to make out a little in my bunk?" Jeremy asks.

I let out a yawn, and reach my arms out to stretch. "Sorry, I'm so tired, and I've got another early-morning flight tomorrow."

"No problem. Don't be disappointed by what I said earlier, alright? I do love you, you know," Jeremy says as we stand up.

He steps over to me and wraps his arms around me, pulling me close to him. "When the time's right, Elena, I'll be more than happy to have a baby with you. Just, not yet."

I sigh, but at least he's not dismissing the idea completely. After another kiss goodbye, I head back to my quarters.

My tummy is still feeling kind of weird, but maybe it's just been a tough day. Or the feta cheese isn't sitting well, one of the two.

Chapter 4: Something's Not Right

My alarm beeps making me groan as I open my eyes.

"Ohhhh," I groan again. Something doesn't feel right with me at all.

I hit the panel on my bunk to turn on the light, and as I look down between my swollen boobs, I notice my belly is sticking up by probably two inches.

Damn, I'm *super* bloated! Could it still be from last night's dinner? But I've had the cafeteria's Greek food before, and it never made me feel like this.

I shift out of my bunk and step into the bathroom. Turning sideways, I lift up my black pajama t-shirt.

Man, if I didn't know better, I'd almost guess that I'm three months pregnant?

But no, I *couldn't* be. Could I? With *aliens?* Most women don't even get pregnant the first time they have sex with a guy, and I doubt aliens would be any more biologically compatible with human women than human guys are.

My boobs are also noticeably bigger than they used to be, by maybe even as much as two full cup sizes. Maybe I've just gained some weight? But if so, that's extremely fast. And the discomfort in my abdomen feels more like period cramps than indigestion. Yet it's not the right week for that.

Maybe it really is just gas, combined with hunger? Like last night, I'm totally starving again. I'll need to shower fast and make sure I can get a proper breakfast today before our second day of exploring.

*   *   *

I'm definitely feeling a bit self-conscious about my bloated tummy now that I'm wearing my skin-tight shiny blue unitard. But damn, I'm *hungry!* I step through the wide cafeteria doors and get quickly into a line for my favourite protein smoothie.

As soon as I shut off the smoothie dispenser, I pop the clear lid onto the metal cup, insert a stainless-steel straw, and hurry over to a long white table where Emma, Karlie, and Jessica are seated and chatting. I wouldn't say that they're my best friends, but they're the closest friends I've got on this ship.

Hoping that they don't notice my bulging tummy, I take my seat while sipping on my smoothie.

"Hey Elena. How was the site where your team landed yesterday?"

"Good," I say. "It was great to just relax by the shuttle, enjoy the nice weather and take in the gorgeous scenery."

"Yeah? Sounds nice. But maybe you really should try to exercise a little more instead of just sitting around down there doing nothing. It looks like you're gaining weight," Karlie points out. The others who are smart enough to not be as blunt as she is still nod their heads in agreement.

Fuck, they've noticed. I guess I'll play along, since there's no way I'm going to mention that I might be pregnant after fucking three aliens yesterday.

"Haha, yeah, uh, maybe Doctor Jeremy was right after all, huh?" I say with a smile, even though my cheeks are becoming warm. "I'm sure he won't mind my bigger tits, though, right?" I joke as I put my hands on either side of my boobs and jiggle them. The others laugh.

"So what was it like at Beta team's site?" Jessica asks Emma, and I'm glad it takes the attention off of me.

"Oh, it was awful. It was practically a swamp, and then it started raining. Those waterproof environmental suits are so unbreathable that when we got back I felt like I'd been in a sauna," Emma complains. "Hopefully it won't be raining again today."

"Speaking of that, we'd better finish up and go grab our gear," Karlie says.

We all get up and leave our empty dishes and cups on the racks for them to be washed, then head out of the cafeteria. My friends branch off down the corridor toward their laboratories to get their gear, and I continue on toward the shuttlebay to do my pre-flight checks.

At least when I'm seated and strapped into my pilot's seat it somewhat hides my bulging tummy. Hopefully none of the research team will notice.

*   *   *

I breathe a sigh of relief when the team clears out of the shuttle and Gerald the lead researcher begins giving his daily instructions to his team. He'd been so distracted with examining his data on his tablet that he didn't even notice my slightly larger belly. Now that they're all clearing out, I can get out of my seat an exit the shuttle.

The day is a little cooler and more cloudy, so at least I'm not burning up as much as I was yesterday. But *man*, my belly is feeling so uncomfortable!

I just stand here and run my hands over it several times. If it's gas, this is the most bloated I've ever been. I'm sure I still look three months pregnant, and that annoying dull ache is still there deep inside. But now, my skin is feeling kind of tight, too.

Just to check, I face the lake and zip down my unitard. My belly's skin actually looks a little bit more pink than it was this morning. Is it stretching? Is that why it feels tight?

And look at my nipples! Each one's areola is even darker pink than it was yesterday after the aliens finished sucking on them, and my nipples stick out farther than ever before.

Well, I definitely don't want to risk anyone seeing me like this today. If it stays cool enough I'll just stay in the shuttle and monitor the sensors.

*   *   *

The shuttle's chronometer shows 14:56, so the research team should be back in half an hour, at most.

But I'm just going to sit here, since my belly seems to be protruding at least an inch or two more than it was this morning. That inner ache is intensifying, and I've been massaging my belly for the last hour or so, trying to make it feel better.

However, the longer this goes on, and the larger I seem to be growing, the more I'm leaning toward the idea that those three aliens really did impregnate me.

But if I'm pregnant, I don't have any idea what to do. Surely, if I keep getting bigger at this same rate, I won't be able to hide this from the crew for long. The captain will notice, and so will Jeremy. And then I'll be in so much trouble.

Several large leaves at the edge of the overgrown jungle off to the right move, and I watch two of our team trudge out from the jungle in their protective environmental suits. Okay, so, only an hour more, and I'll be back on board my ship. I'll wait to decide what to do until then.

*   *   *

Gerald spins around in the chair beside me and stands up. He takes two steps toward the open hatch at the back of the shuttle, then stops.

"Aren't you coming?" he asks.

"Oh, no. I'm going to run a few extra maintenance tests on the shuttle," I say without turning around.

"Sounds good, see you again tomorrow," he says, and I hear his footsteps leave the shuttle.

I breathe a sigh of relief. Good thing he was so wrapped up in going over his new data during the flight back that he didn't notice my belly. I probably look like I'm about six months pregnant by now!

Just to make sure the shuttle's logs match with my little fib, I sit for an extra twenty minutes and run a few automated tests. The results all come back good, like I expected. The Beta team's shuttle has also landed and the research team unloaded and cleared out of the shuttlebay, so hopefully everyone is back dropping off their equipment in the laboratories, and I can make it to my quarters without running into anyone in the corridors.

Taking a deep breath, I spin my chair around and stand up for the first time in four hours. Man, it feels like I've gained fifteen pounds!

I really need to get back to my quarters and check myself out more thoroughly. The large shuttlebay door whooshes apart, and I step into the empty corridor beyond it.

Knowing that anyone who sees me will clearly see that something's not right with me, I try to walk as quickly as I can. There's definitely an unusual sensation of weight in my belly, and my hope that this is just bloating vanishes. I simply *must* be pregnant—it's the only thing that makes sense.

Going around each corner or intersection in the corridors makes my heart fill with dread at the thought of seeing someone. Fortunately, I'm soon at my quarters, and I run the last few steps to hit the button and open my door.

The lights automatically turn on as I step inside, and the door hisses shut behind me. I set the privacy lock and take several deep breaths to try to calm my racing heart.

I quickly take off my stretchy blue unitard and leave it on the ground. Stepping into my bathroom in just my panties, I inspect my reflection.

Fuck. My belly sticks out probably *twice* as far as it did this morning! And my belly's skin is still rather pink-tinged, as if it's struggling to keep up with my womb's rapid expansion.

I run my hands over my curved belly. If this was Jeremy's baby in me, I'd be thrilled. But now, I'm just feeling uncertain, and anxious at the thought of having an alien baby growing in me. Or maybe even more than one. At this point it's the only answer that makes any sense.

But if this is only the second day of my pregnancy, how big am I going to get before I'm ready to give birth? If it's nine whole months, I might be *huge* by then! What if I get so big I can't sit in the pilot's seat anymore? What if I can't even fit in my *bunk?*

Even worse, what will Jeremy think of me? And what will Captain Kriger do?

Feeling like I'm on the verge of tears, I take another breath, and try to calm down. Panicking won't help. Maybe my situation just seems worse since I'm still famished, like I've been all day.

I sit down on the edge of my bunk, spreading my legs to give some room for the bottom of my bulging tummy. I grab my personal tablet and check my messages. Nothing from Jeremy, so maybe he's busy. Or he wants some space, in case he's worried I might pester him with more questions about our future.

However, there's no way I want to go to the cafeteria like this. Maybe I'll send Jeremy a message and see if he can bring me some take-out.

Hey babe, I'm exhausted, but totally famished. Can you grab me some dinner and bring it to my quarters? I send.

Sure, be there in ten minutes, he replies.

Okay, good, but how do I hide my enlarging tummy from him? Turning my head, I notice my black pajamas laying on my bunk next to me. At least they're loose- fitting than my unitard, and the dark color might hide my bump.

Slipping on my pajama shorts and matching t-shirt, I'm satisfied. The top is a little tighter across my mid-section, but if I dim the lights in my quarters, Jeremy might not notice.

*   *   *

The door beeps, and I know he's here. I take a deep breath, and stand up, taking two steps to the door. I reach for the button to de-activate the privacy lock, then cross my arms over my belly to hide it a little more, just in time for the door to open.

"Hey babe," I say with the biggest smile I can. Jeremy is standing there with two take-out containers of food. Immediately, I reach for the top one. "Thanks so much, I'm so hungry," I say, and hold the container just below my boobs where it should shield his view of my bulging belly.

"Yeah?" he replies. "You feeling alright? You haven't seemed like yourself these last two days. We can go to the medical bay and I'll give you a few scans, if you want? If it's all good, how about we go to the rec center and have some fun?"

"Oh no, no, I'm fine. It must just be the heat down there on the planet," I lie. "It just makes me so hungry and tired. I think I'll get to sleep early. But you should go, have a good time," I say.

"Suit yourself. Have a good night, Elena," he says. He leans forward to give me a kiss, and I return it, before giving him one last smile. When he turns, I hit the privacy lock button to shut the door as fast as I can.

I know he's right—I *have* been acting funny lately. Hopefully my excuse will satisfy him.

At least if I can eat now, and hopefully get a good sleep, I'll be able to think more clearly tomorrow morning about what to do about my apparent alien pregnancy predicament.

Chapter 5: I Want More!

I look down at the coarse reddish-orange sand below my feet. To my left is my shuttle, which I must've flown down. But there's no research team here with me, and I recognize the same pool surrounded by cliffs with the waterfall where I'd fucked the aliens.

But why am I here again? I just can't remember.

Fortunately, I look down at myself, and my stomach is flat. I'm not pregnant, and sudden relief washes over me. However, I begin to hear many, many sounds of the aliens' unusual melodic language.

I look up and see not just three, but maybe *a dozen* teal-skinned muscular aliens all walking fast across the sandy shore toward me. But behind them, even *more* aliens are streaming out from behind the waterfall. Soon, there's probably seventy or even eighty sexy male aliens on the beach walking toward me, and more just keep coming!

Every one of them has a massive teal erection. Do they think I'm here to fuck them again? *Am* I here to fuck them again?

Their strong alien bodies turn me on more than I can understand, and I instantly know that yes, I want them *all*.

The horde of tall teal aliens quickly surround me, and their large six-fingered hands begin to touch me all over. One of them finds my unitard zipper and pulls it down. The others help undress me, and soon I'm totally naked.

Bulging teal-skinned muscles surround me on every side, and I take two thick penises into my hands to begin to jerk them off. I kneel down and take a third alien cock into my mouth, and start sucking on it, even while stroking the other two aliens penises.

Strong alien hands grip my hips and legs, and suddenly they lift me up! But my head remains at the height of the alien's groin, and his cock is still in my mouth.

The aliens spread my legs, exposing my wet pussy to them. Then the one whose dick I'm sucking suddenly pulls back, and together, all the aliens flip my body over, even though they're still all holding me up above the beach.

The aliens on either side of me instantly bend over and place their O-shaped mouths over each of my nipples. They start to suck on them, even while the aliens directly behind me holds my body up.

As the aliens suck on my boobs, I'm amazed to watch my breasts begin to enlarge. But I can still see between them, at least for now, so I watch the alien who is standing between my legs lean forward.

"Ohhhhh," I groan, as his massive erection instantly penetrates me and fills my entire vagina.

Since I'm feeling very supported by all the alien hands that are holding me up, I reach out and grasp two more of their cocks, one in each of my hands. The alien whose penis is in my pussy begins to thrust, and the entire crowd of aliens begins making almost a symphony of their strange little musical tones.

I can totally hear the alien's gigantic cock sliding back and forth between my wet folds, and I'm so extremely turned on. There's no way Jeremy would ever measure up to these extremely masculine, super-sexy aliens. I'd better fuck as many of them as I can now, before we have to leave the planet.

"Yeah, oh, that's perfect," I say.

The alien picks up the speed of his thrusting, and soon he's absolutely pounding me! I feel like I'm loose enough that I've somehow taken his entire massive cock into me, and I love how much his girth is stretching my walls. His weighty balls slap against my pussy, and I know it won't be long until—

"Aaaaaoooooo!" he howls louder than I've ever heard. It rings in my ears as I feel a pulse pass up the length of his shaft and explode in my uterus.

"Yes, YES! Oh, oh yeah. Fuck me! Fill me up!" I scream.

The two alien cocks in each of my hands also pulse, and the first alien's howl is joined by two more. They let loose and two thick ropes of alien cum shoot out of their urethras. The alien cum splashes up over my collarbones and neck, even while the two aliens sucking on my nipples don't seem to care at all.

Suddenly, the alien in my pussy pulls his cock out, and in less than a second, another massive teal alien penis is filling my hole.

"Oh yeah, yeah! MORE!" I scream, as the next alien urgently pounds me. In only seconds, he too is howling and cumming in my womb.

Looking down between my huge breasts, each one of which is likely the size of the bowling balls in the ship's rec center, I notice my belly begin to bulge.

I grab two new alien cocks, and begin to jerk them off too, even while the third alien takes his place in my pussy.

Oh, I could just do this forever! The pleasure they're bringing me is totally amazing! Even though my belly is rapidly getting larger and larger as one alien after another releases all their cum into me, I don't want this to stop.

But my belly continues to grow. I'm feeling myself get heavier and heavier, and soon, the aliens lay me down on the sand. Yet the seventh alien howls as he ejaculates his potent cum into my womb, and the fifth double-dose of alien semen flows across my collarbones.

Surely, there's more than just cum in me, though. My belly has rapidly expanded to the point where I must look like I'm eighteen months pregnant, if this were a normal human pregnancy. Just how many alien babies are in me? And how many will be in me by the time this entire massive horde of aliens has finished with me?

Oh, but I want more! MORE! I want to be *huge!* Who cares if I end up with four dozen alien babies in me at once? I just want to fuck these aliens forever!

"Ah, oh, Oh! OH yes! Impregnate me, all of you!" I cry out, and throw my head backward.

An alien cock pushes itself down my throat, and I start sucking on it, even while I know my belly is growing faster and becoming bigger than I could ever imagine.

The alien cock in my mouth pulses and spews out a blast of cum, but I can't drink it fast enough! It's leaking out of my mouth and down my chin, and I can barely catch my breath—

I sit up and gasp, but my forehead bumps into the padded top of my bunk in my dark quarters.

A dream, it was only a dream. I reach out to the panel in my bunk to turn on the lights, but then I notice it: my belly really *is* huge!

Chapter 6: Too Big to Hide

"Uh oh," I mumble as I run my hands over the large warm mound that's now my belly. The top of my tummy almost touches the top of my bunk.

I'm nowhere near as large as I got in my dream, but I'm definitely way bigger than I was when I went to bed. I must look like I'm a full-term human pregnancy, and *then* some!

Easing myself sideways, I manage to squeeze my huge pregnant belly out of my bunk, and set my feet on the floor.

Rushing into my bathroom, the lights turn on, and I stare at myself with wide eyes and mouth hanging open. If I didn't know better, I really *would* think I'm ready to deliver sextuplets any minute now!

My black t-shirt is bunched up above my belly and stretched as it tries to contain my boobs, which also have grown significantly overnight. I pull my shirt off and drop it on the floor, and stare at the truly bowling-ball sized breasts that are resting on top of my belly. My areolas are so large and dark, and my nipples stick out by a full inch, each one as thick as my pinky finger. Not surprisingly, my new super-sized boobs are also a little achy.

The sight of me with this massive pregnant belly and enormous breasts makes my clit twinge. When I turn to the side and check myself out, it twinges again. I've never felt so sexy, even though my belly feels like it weighs probably thirty pounds, and my boobs are likely ten pounds each.

Oh, but what do I *do?* There's no way I'll be able to hide this huge belly from everyone now.

What time is it? I step back out into my quarters and check the time on my bunk chronometer. 04:43. Okay, so I don't need to be down in the shuttlebay anytime soon.

It occurs to me that I really only have one option: I need to go to the medical bay.

Not wanting to walk through the ship topless like this, and realizing that if I bend over to grab my pajama top I might not be able to stand back up, I pull open the laundry drawer just below my bunk. My unitard is in there, clean and dry, so I'll try that.

Reaching behind me, I manage to pull my pajama shorts down over my ass, and they drop to the floor. Now I slip my right foot through the unzipped front of my unitard, and manage to find the right leg.

I huff and puff as I struggle to wiggle my foot down through the stretchy fabric, but I soon feel the sole of the built-in shoe is in place. Okay, same thing for the left foot.

With some effort, I pull the rest of the unitard up over my butt and slip my arms down the arm holes. I feel around below my belly for the zipper, and start to pull it upward.

Luckily, the stretchy fabric manages to accommodate my body's new shape well enough, and the zipper does close my unitard even over the top of my huge pregnant belly.

The door to my quarters opens, and I dare to step through into the hallway. I can't believe how large the corridor lights make my belly look in this shiny blue fabric. What would my friends say if they could see me like this? Yet since it's early in the morning, there doesn't seem to be anyone in the corridors.

Although my heart is beating fast and I've got adrenaline coursing through me, it takes noticeably more effort to move my body than it did yesterday.

I begin to head for the medical bay, but then I realize that if everyone else is still sleeping, then Jeremy won't be in the medical bay, either. I should go to his quarters and wake him up.

"Ugggg," I groan, as I stop and turn around, then lumber back in the opposite direction.

After probably twice as long as usual, I'm standing in front of Jeremy's quarters, breathing heavily.

The button is right there. With a sweaty finger, I push it a few times, as dread fills my stomach.

My heart leaps as the door to Jeremy's quarters opens, revealing a dim interior and Jeremy in his black pajama shorts and top, rubbing his eyes and yawning. But as soon as he sees me, his eyes go wide open.

"Elena? What… what *is* this? You're *pregnant?*"

"Shhh, can I come inside?" I ask.

"Yeah," he replies, and steps out of the way. I enter his quarters, and am relieved to hear the door shut behind me.

"But why are you so *pregnant?*" Jeremy asks. "You weren't pregnant yesterday."

I hang my head, and my cheeks feel like they're on fire. "Actually, I was. I think I got pregnant just under two days ago," I say, trying not to look him in the eyes.

"But you're *huge!* No woman gets that big that fast," he says.

"Um, well, most women haven't had sex with aliens, either," I say quietly, still too ashamed to look at him. Instead, I just run my hands over my huge belly under my stretched unitard.

"Aliens? *Aliens?* As in, more than one alien? Elena, you're not making sense!" Jeremy starts to pace back and forth as he runs his fingers through his dark curly hair.

"It's true, babe. Um, the first day we were down on the new planet, I told you I went for a swim, right? Well, I also met three sexy aliens, and I was just so horny, and curious, and their dicks were huge, so…"

"What? Elena, baby, no. No. You *didn't!*"

"I'm so sorry Jeremy! I thought no one would ever know. But now, just look at me. What do we *do?*" My eyes fill with tears, and I begin to cry.

"Oh, oh, baby, just come with me, let's get you to the medical bay." Jeremy wraps his arm around my waist, and I turn around. He opens the door to his quarters, and begins to usher me through the ship's corridors toward the medical bay. He didn't even get dressed, and is just walking barefoot in his pajama shorts and top.

However, I'm already feeling like it's taking me more effort to walk back from Jeremy's quarters than it did to get to them. Is my belly growing larger, even now?

Finally, the doors to the medical bay hiss apart, and we step inside. Jeremy guides me toward the nearest medical bed, and it requires all my strength to hop up onto it.

The display behind me automatically turns on and I hear fast little beeps that match with my heart rate. Jeremy goes away into his office and comes back wearing his medical coat over his pajamas, and is carrying one of his handheld medical scanners.

The scanner begins to beep softly as he passes it over my huge pregnant belly. He looks up at the display above my head, and blinks several times. Then he repeats the scan twice more.

"What is it? What's in me?" I ask, somewhat nervous about what he'll say.

"Uh, it looks like eggs," he says.

"*Eggs?!*" I ask, as my eyes fly wide open and my jaw drops. "You said I've got *alien eggs* in my womb?"

"Over five hundred, actually," he says.

"WHAT?!" I shout. "But if it's just eggs, why are my boobs so big? And they're starting to ache, too," I complain.

"Can you unzip your unitard?" he asks.

"Okay," I say, and do. As I pull the zipper down my huge boobs spill out, soon followed by the top of my oversized pregnant belly. Jeremy helps me take the zipper down the rest of the way, until both my boobs and belly are fully exposed.

Damn, my round stomach is probably ten percent larger than it was when I woke up!

I reach up and cup my huge boobs and start to massage them. This helps a little bit, but I can't get my hands around more than a quarter of each one.

Suddenly, I feel the weirdest dripping sensation inside each of my boobs.

"I, I feel something. In my boobs," I say, but keep massaging them.

Before I can do anything, several streams of milk spray out from each nipple. With each squeeze, more milk comes out of my breasts, and begins dripping down the underside of my boobs.

"Jeremy! What's happening to me?!" I exclaim.

"Shhh, shhh," he says. "Don't worry, you're just lactating. It's harmless. It's not surprising, really. The scans here say you've got three times the amount of prolactin and progesterone in your body than is usual for a typical pregnant woman."

"Oh, great," I mumble.

"Look, Elena, you're otherwise healthy, but there's no way you're fit for duty. I'll have to inform Captain Kriger that you won't be flying anywhere today. However, I think we can still keep your infraction a secret. I'll prep you for surgery, and we can take out those eggs and dispose of them. Then, I'll tell the captain that it was just an unnaturally fast-growing tumor. Once you're recovered, then—"

"*Surgery?*" I gasp. "But, do I have to?"

"Unless you want to keep those eggs in you, and see exactly how big you get, it's the only option."

I admit, the idea makes my clit twinge a few times. Realistically, I know it's probably not a good idea, but I've always been terrified of undergoing surgery. The time I had to have my appendix out as a kid gave me nightmares for months afterward.

"Can't we wait just a little longer? In case they stop growing, and are ready to, uh, come out naturally?" I ask.

"Elena, I don't think that's a good idea," Jeremy says. "Just look at how fast you've grown already. And according to my scans, that rate is increasing. I'm actually amazed that your body has handled it as well as it has."

"I don't want to have surgery," I pout.

Jeremy sighs. "Look, I'm going to go wake up Captain Kriger. He needs to know. Just stay here, and we can decide after that."

Jeremy turns and leaves the medical bay.

Tears begin to well up in my eyes. If Captain Kriger finds out, he'll probably demote me since I didn't report that I'd made contact with aliens, and I also majorly broke the rules by fucking them. He probably won't let me fly anymore, and Jeremy will surely break up with me, too.

Then it occurs to me: maybe I should leave? I don't know where I'd go, but if I don't want surgery, now's the time to make a break for it.

Chapter 7: Time to Go

With a groan, I reach around my huge belly. My fingers find the zipper, and I manage to pull it up over myself to close my unitard. Then I slide my butt off the medical bed, and head out of the medical bay.

I wrap my arms under my extremely heavy stomach to give it some support, and lumber off in the direction of the shuttlebay as fast as I can manage.

As I go, I'm hearing tiny little clicks. More clicks occur, until suddenly my unitard's zipper fails, each side pulling apart from the other. Thanks to the stretchy fabric, my huge egg-filled belly comes out, and the zipper even separates across my enormous breasts.

But I don't have time to stop and try to fix it now. I just keep going even through my leaking breasts and giant belly are in full view of anyone who might come down the corridor.

By the time I pass through the shuttlebay doors I'm huffing and puffing quite strongly, and my legs are quivering with exertion. I head directly for my shuttle, and waddle up the lowered rear ramp and through the rear hatch. I suspect my pregnant tummy is about two feet in diameter!

Streams of milk are leaking down my breasts as I spin my pilot's seat around and get in. When I rotate the seat forward, my huge belly presses up against the bottom of the pilot's console, but I still manage to strap myself in.

Fuck the pre-flight checks, I'm just gonna power this thing up, close the hatch, and initiate the auto-launch signal that will open the shuttlebay doors. Everything else I can do on the way down to the planet.

Now I know where I need to go. The aliens deserve to have their eggs. Plus, the aliens should have more knowledge about what an alien pregnancy is like than Jeremy does.

In only minutes, I'm ready to go. My shuttle lifts up, spins around, and smoothly glides right out the open bay doors. However, I'm sure my unauthorized use of a shuttle means this is likely the last flight of my career.

I direct the shuttle toward the planet, and bring up the same landing site that we've used the last two days. Even though I'm somewhat distracted by my belly and lactating breasts, I manage to focus on entering the planet's atmosphere just fine.

Instead of landing in the same spot as before, I fly low, following the shore of the lake around the mountain while looking for the waterfall. When I find it, I set down my shuttle as close to the waterfall as I can. However, I don't see any aliens out and about. The planet's sun is lower and beginning to set, but fortunately it's behind me and isn't blocked by the cliffs.

I lower the rear hatch, spin around in my chair, and power off the shuttle. It takes all my effort and my legs strain as I lift myself up out of my seat, wrap my arms under my belly, and lumber out the shuttle's open rear hatch.

Leaning back as far as I can to keep my new center of gravity over my feet, I slowly make my way across the coarse reddish-orange sand toward the waterfall. Presumably, there must be a cave or something behind there that the aliens live in? Otherwise, I don't see how they could have appeared so suddenly when I was swimming.

As I get closer, the spray from the waterfall sprinkles cool drops over my exposed belly and breasts, but I keep going. It looks like there's a small path behind it, and— ah ha, there *is* a cave entrance!

I waddle up to the entrance of a mostly natural-looking cave, but I do see some marks that look like part of the rock has been chiselled away. This must be the right spot.

"Hello?" I call out as loudly as I can. "Anyone home?" My voice echoes inside.

Screw it, I'm going in. The light from the setting sun shining into the entryway lets me see at least a little ways into the cave, but the rocks are slightly slippery from moisture from the waterfall, so I go carefully.

"Hello? Sexy aliens? Are you here?" I shout, as ridiculous as that sounds.

A faint series of little tones is literal music to my ears. From a dark passage off in the back of the larger cave I see two large teal-skinned aliens appear.

As soon as they see me, they rush over to me. I guess they must be the same ones I fucked earlier, since they don't seem overly shocked. Right away they fasten their O-shaped mouths over my nipples and start sucking.

"Oh yes, that's good," I say. Even though my belly seems to be getting heavier and larger with every passing minute, I just let the aliens drink as much milk from me as they want. As they do, my boobs begin to not ache so much.

A third alien appears soon, and he too comes over to me. He starts rubbing his teal six-fingered hands over my belly, while serenading me with a little tune. I guess he's happy?

He pushes against the biceps of the other two aliens, who stop sucking on my tits. The first alien turns around and the other two link their arms with mine as they escort me deeper into their caves.

I'm worried as the cave gets darker and darker, but my eyes manage to adjust to the dim light. They lead me through a few different rocky chambers, and a corridor with a surprisingly smooth floor gradually leads uphill. They must have chiselled this passageway out themselves with whatever simple tools they have.

Finally, they lead me into a relatively large chamber. A hole in the center of the rocky ceiling allows a shaft of light to enter. Three niches are hollowed into the cave walls, but they're empty except for a few flattened piles of moss. Is this where they sleep?

The aliens lead me over to the unoccupied niche to my left. Before I can sit down, the two aliens next to me begin to tug on the sides of my open unitard.

"Sure, take it off, I don't mind," I say, and try to help them as best I can. They also help me take off my panties.

Now fully naked, they take my hands and turn me away from the center of the room, so that I'm facing the wall of the niche. They motion downward with their hands, so I squat down and gratefully rest my naked butt on the cushioning pile of moss.

I spread my legs and let my three-foot diameter belly rest on the floor between my thighs, while leaning forward and resting my head on top of my boobs, which are themselves resting on my belly.

At least I feel like I'm in good hands here with the aliens. But surely it won't be long until Captain Kriger discovers where I've gone.

*   *   *

Over the last several hours the aliens have tried to make conversation with me without any success. I wouldn't even know where to start learning their language. After all, I'm a pilot, not a linguist.

Even though I'm totally naked, it's almost the perfect temperature in here. The tropical air outside must filter in and keep the small cavern room warm, but not too warm.

The three sexy male aliens are certainly taking good care of me. A little while after I arrived they brought in some sort of paste that smelled like berries, and they rubbed it all over my belly. It dried up and flaked off as my tummy grew, but it really did make my skin feel a lot better.

Eventually they also brought me a selection of delicious fresh fruit, and some water in a clay jug. I've eaten as much as I can, and I'm finally feeling full.

But my belly has just continued to grow, and it doesn't show any signs of stopping soon. I suspect my belly is currently over four feet in diameter. Based on how heavy it was when I came into the cave, I know there's no way I could hope to stand up now.

Even though I'm happy that Captain Kriger or Jeremy haven't shown up yet, I can't stop worrying about what will happen when they do.

Chapter 8: Egg Delivery

"Hmm?" I mumble drowsily as my eyes open. I hear footsteps of the three aliens behind me, and they're also making a repetitive little noise as if they're waking me up. But it's far more pleasant than my alarm clock ever was.

The ambient light in the cavern room is once again becoming bright, so it must be early morning.

Yet I'm shocked by how big my belly is. Although I've managed to shift my position so that I'm now kneeling at the edge of the pile of squishy moss, the massive spherical surface of my egg-filled belly rises up off the smooth stone floor by probably six feet!

I groan, and use all my strength to roll my belly slightly forward so that I can stand up. It's truly bizarre how big my stomach has grown, but I'm really not in any discomfort.

Two aliens step up to either side of me, and I notice them looking eagerly at my boobs.

"You guys want some breakfast?" I ask, and cup my hands on either side of my breasts, each of which has become twelve inches in diameter. I jostle them a little, and the warm dribble that I feel from my nipples tells me just how full of milk my boobs must be after that full night's sleep.

The two aliens plant their O-shaped lips right over my nipples. Now that I'm lactating, their sucking feels even better than it did when we had sex out on the alien's beach.

Their rhythmic sucking makes my vagina pulse, and I know I'm getting wet. However, my truly enormous belly shows that I'm in no position to be having sex with them anytime soon.

After what I'd guess has been twenty minutes, the aliens stop sucking on my boobs. They also bring me some fruit, and several more jugs of water. I'm so thirsty I motion for the water, and they pass it to me.

While I'm drinking, I hear the familiar sound of shuttlecraft engines overhead. It fades only a little, then shuts off. Okay, so, Captain Kriger and Jeremy must have held off coming during the night and waited for first light to come find me.

The aliens who are tending to me look up, and then rush out of the room. All I hope is that Captain Kriger has enough sense to not get into a violent confrontation with them.

It takes longer than I expected, but soon I hear several pairs of boots clomping down the stone hallway outside. This is accompanied by many high-pitched loud noises from the aliens, who must not be too happy.

I crane my neck to look back over my shoulder, and watch one alien, followed by Captain Kriger, Jeremy, and two security officers holding laser-rifles enter the cave room. The other two aliens enter the room after them.

Even though the aliens are big enough that they'd surely win in a physical fight, they seem to know better than to try anything with the guards there.

"Elena, there you are. But, you're *massive!* How…"

Jeremy goes silent as he stares at my naked body standing here in front of my six-foot diameter belly. Then he begins to rub at his groin, where I see the outline of his erection under his tight stretchy unitard.

"Hey, Jeremy," I say, and give him a smile.

"Lieutenant Elena, this is truly unacceptable," Captain Kriger says in his stern voice. He crosses his arms over his chest, and scowls at me.

But it's not like there's anything he can do to change the situation. I'm here, in the aliens' caves, massively pregnant, and unable to go anywhere until I give birth to the alien eggs that are in my belly.

"How could you have done such a thing?" Captain Kriger begins to lecture me, as he paces back and forth in the small room.

"First, you dared to have sex with strange alien men, which is completely *not* our protocol for encountering intelligent alien life. Then, you didn't report the existence of these aliens to our research team. Next, you took an *unbelievable* risk by hiding your alien pregnancy, and finally, you disregarded the doctor's orders, stole a shuttle, and came back to interfere even more with the aliens! You're hereby stripped of your rank, and permanently assigned to shuttle maintenance duties for the rest of our mission. Once we arrive back on Earth, you'll be dishonorably discharged, and perhaps even held criminally liable for your actions."

Although I should be sad about this, I've had enough of his lecturing.

"Yeah? Well, Captain, first you're gonna have to get me out of here. And I'm not going anywhere anytime soon, as I think you can see, and— ohhh," I suddenly moan, as a strange contraction ripples through my massive belly.

I just stop and pay close attention to what I'm feeling. Is it the stress of all this that's triggered some cramps inside my womb? Or has it just so happened that it's time for me to give birth?

Another cramp occurs, and there's a dull ache that's increasing in intensity which must be from my cervix starting to dilate.

"What is it, Lieutenant?" the captain demands.

"Sorry, I, I think I'm going into labor!"

I gasp, as another, stronger cramp passes through my extremely stretched uterus. "Ohhh," I moan.

The three stronger, larger aliens quickly push past the captain and his guards and take their places all around my belly, one at the front, and two at the sides. They all begin to massage my enormous pregnant belly with their six spread fingers with bulbous tips. It actually feels pretty good, but it also makes the eggs inside me jostle around.

I press in on my belly, and sure enough, there's many hard bumps just under the surface of my skin. I can't tell for sure how big they are, but they're not an unreasonable size. Hopefully they'll come out just fine. At least Jeremy is carrying his portable medical kit, in case it turns out that surgery is unavoidable.

"Labor! I don't give you permission to go into labor, Lieutentant!" the captain shouts.

"Sir, calm down," Jeremy says. "Don't stress her any more than she needs to be. Please step over there while I monitor her delivery," he says to the captain and his guards.

The captain harumphs, but does what Jeremy instructed. Both security guards stare at me with wide eyes and their mouths hanging open, and lower their rifles toward the ground.

The feeling of all these eggs shifting around inside me does distract me from the strengthening ache in my dilating cervix. Yet the pressure of the eggs jostling against it from the inside is helping distract me from it somewhat.

It occurs to me that I might need some lubrication to help these eggs slide out of me.

"Here, suck on my boobs," I say. The aliens turn to look at me, and see me pointing at my nipples. Two of them move to place their O-lipped mouths over my nipples and start sucking, while the third uses all his strength to keep massaging my gigantic egg-filled tummy.

"Can the security guards help massage me like the aliens were doing?" I ask, as I crane my neck around to look at Captain Kriger.

"Hmmph. Fine. Get to it, men," he says.

The two security guys look at each other, then at me, and rush over to either side of me. They're tentative at first, but soon they're putting all their strength into it, and it feels amazing.

All the motion of the eggs inside my belly means I can actually see slight bumps moving under the surface of my skin as the eggs jostle around inside my womb. Well that's a sight I never expected to see! Yet it's also really turning me on. Either that, or it's the wonderful sensation of the two aliens sucking milk out of my enormous tits that's making my pussy wet, my clit twinge, and my vagina start clenching.

The pressure deep inside me is getting stronger, and stronger, until it's almost unbearable!

"Uhhhh, ohhh, *ohhhhh*..." I begin to groan.

When I think it can't get any worse, I feel sudden relief, as well as the sensation of a large object occupying my vagina.

"Oh, I think it's coming through!" I shout, as I bear down with all my strength.

74

The egg moves downward, probably assisted by gravity as well as my now-well-lubricated channel. However, there's still quite a lot of stretching going on in there as my pussy loosens up.

"Uhhh, oh, ohhhh," I moan, as I squeeze my vagina with all the strength I've got. However, just then *another* object passes through my cervix. I've got two eggs in my pussy at once!

The extra weight of the second egg helps the first egg press even harder against my vaginal entrance, and I feel like it's slowly stretching me wider and wider.

"Ohhhhh," I groan loudly and squeeze with everything I've got. Two large waves of pressure pass through my hole, and I hear a dull thud as both eggs land in the mossy bed below me.

"She's laying *eggs?!*" the captain exclaims. Didn't Jeremy tell him that part?

"Yeah, oh, but there's more coming," I moan. Another two eggs have already taken their places in my birth canal, and again, I try to bear down on them as hard as I can.

"Unnnnnggghh," I groan, but the two eggs drop out of me easier than the first two did.

I hear commotion behind me as Jeremy rushes over and kneels down behind me. He rustles the mossy pile a little, maybe to make a nest to keep the eggs from rolling away, and then I feel his hands between my upper thighs.

Although my pussy is again full of two eggs, which seems to be all that can fit in it at once, I'm feeling that I'm loosening up already. This time, I try just a little squeeze, and as I'd intended, just one alien egg drops out of me and into Jeremy's waiting hands.

"Got, it," he says, and looks up at me with a smile.

I smile back at him over my shoulder, and put the same amount of pressure on the next egg. It drops out likewise, and now after six eggs, I think I'm getting the hang of this.

I begin to lay one egg after the other, and the rate the aliens' eggs are coming out of me is slowly increasing as I become increasingly loose, and also as I'm getting totally turned on.

All these men here, watching me lay alien eggs, with my gigantic lactating boobs and my truly enormous belly is just so fucking *hot!*

As my belly slowly begins to empty, there becomes even more room for the remaining eggs to jostle around inside my womb. Yet they keep finding their way through my cervix, and it takes hardly any effort on my part other than a gentle push to pop each egg out of my pussy. I think I'm down to one egg per second!

The wonderful feelings of the aliens sucking milk out of my boobs while I'm giving birth to their eggs is just incredible. I'm even starting to enjoy the sensation of the eggs rolling through my cervix, down my tunnel, and popping out of my vagina, one after the other.

Oh yes, this is amazing! I never *imagined* I could feel so much pleasure at once.

Each egg massages my tunnel as it passes through me, and it almost feels like a truly massive penis-knob pulling out of me, over and over. It's even stimulating my clit from the inside, making it twinge and my vagina pulse, which sends another egg out of it.

I've probably laid eighty eggs by now, but didn't Jeremy say I had over five hundred in me?

"Oh, oh yeah, that feels so good!" I gasp as I lay three more eggs.

In a way, it seems my fantasy of being incredibly pregnant has been fulfilled several times over!

Sure, it's not Jeremy's babies, which, if it were, I'd probably have twenty or so inside me at the size I am now. But actually, I totally *love* how insanely huge I am! I also really, really love my giant lactating boobs.

It's too bad this is a once-in-a-lifetime experience, and then Captain Kriger will drag me back up to the ship. But what if... what if I *could* do this again? And then again. And *again!*

A familiar tingling is building up in my core, and my clit twinges several times.

What if I could stay here, be re-impregnated by the aliens, watch my belly grow huge, and lay their eggs every three days? Surely, my boobs would keep on making milk, and the aliens could just fuck me and suck on my tits for hours, out on that gorgeous beach...

"Oh yeah, oh, oh! OH yeah, oh, yes, Yes. YES, OH!" I scream as an orgasm builds up and then overtakes me all at once.

"Yes, yes, yes, yes, yes, YES!" I shout as pleasure surges through me. Every time I shout, an egg pops out of my pussy.

"There's too many!" Jeremy shouts. Captain Kriger rushes over, but there's only so much space between my legs. Instead, I see him start rolling eggs away from Jeremy and into the empty stone niche next to me.

Each round egg is probably three inches in diameter, and is a strange pale turquoise color, halfway between the shade of the water in the lake outside and the teal of the aliens' skin.

Oh, yeah, I could just lay eggs forever—it feels so good!

I keep popping eggs out of me, but my belly is becoming more saggy by the minute as the eggs empty out of it. I'm also becoming somewhat exhausted, so I tap the strong shoulders of the aliens who've been sucking milk out of my tits, and they open their eyes to let go of my nipples.

"Jeremy, I'm gonna kneel down, okay?" He moves out of the way so I can bend down and rest my knees on the moss pile under me, even while I keep passing eggs out of my pussy at a regular rate.

The two aliens who had been drinking from my boobs push the security guards out of the way. The two men step back and climb over the significant pile of eggs behind me until they're out of the way.

Now all three aliens help push the remaining eggs inside my belly back toward my cervix, until I'm left with only a pile of extremely distended loose skin hanging from my torso. It sags down to form a flat pancake shape on the floor of the aliens' cave.

The men behind me have been shoveling the eggs I just laid into the other two niches with their hands and feet, so that there's enough room for me to finally lay down and collapse on top of my enormous flat empty belly and my still-round and amazingly large boobs.

I just breathe deeply and savor the pleasurable hormones that are still coursing through my body after that incredible experience. The aliens make a series of trilling noises, increasing in pitch, over and over. I presume they're thrilled with all the eggs I've laid.

"Alright Lieutenant, now, you're coming with us," Captain Kriger says. I look back over my shoulder just as the two security guards turn and share an uncertain look, before shrugging their shoulders and lifting their laser rifles.

"No, I don't want to go!" I protest. "I want to stay here with the aliens!"

As much fun as it is to fly shuttlecraft, this experience was way better. I feel so proud and accomplished after laying all those eggs, and clearly the aliens seem to like me, so why not?

"No, I can't let you stay. You've interfered with the aliens enough," Captain Kriger says.

"Elena, listen to him," Jeremy begs. "If you come back with us, I'm sure I can do surgery to put your belly back to normal."

But if I didn't want surgery earlier, why on earth would he think I want it now? I don't even care about what's happened to my belly. In fact, if I stay here, I don't think it'll be empty for long. Maybe I'll become even *more* pregnant in the future?

"No, I'm staying here," I say.

"Men, get her, and let's go, now," Captain Kriger orders.

The two security guards step forward and bend down to grab my upper arms, pulling me up and backward, although my heavy stretched belly skin tugs at my abdomen. I grunt and try to wriggle free, but the guards are too strong.

All three aliens let out the loudest howls I've ever heard, and they rush forward. Each large alien easily picks up one of the human security guards, and throws him over their muscular shoulders. The aliens rush out of the room, carrying the captive security guards with them who shout loudly.

The third alien runs at Captain Kriger, who takes a swing at him. The alien dodges it, and punches the captain in his gut.

"Oooof," the Captain wheezes, but the alien has already picked him up and flung him over his shoulder. The alien stops and makes several more angry-sounding noises at Jeremy as he points at the exit to the cave-like room.

"Okay, I'm going, I'm going," Jeremy says. He grabs his medical kit and stands up. "I hope you know what you're doing, Elena," he says as he leaves.

The captain continues to grunt and struggle against the alien, but he's clearly not making any progress at freeing himself. The alien carries him out of the room, and I'm finally left alone in peace.

So, I guess I've got my wish. I'll stay with these aliens, and maybe I'll slowly be able to learn their language, but it doesn't seem like I need to know it. They're clearly capable of taking care of me.

The other pilots can come collect the stolen shuttle, and by then, who knows—maybe my belly will already be filling with even more alien eggs!

THE END

Made in the USA
Las Vegas, NV
05 February 2024

85347495R00049